Farmers Market

Farmers

Carmen Parks

Market

Illustrated by Edward Martinez

Green Light Readers
Harcourt, Inc.
Orlando   Austin   New York   San Diego   Toronto   London

It's still dark, but it's time for me to get up. It's market day in Red Rock.

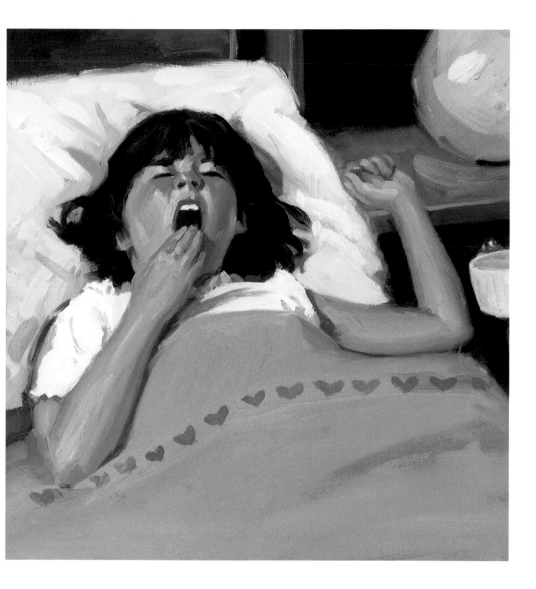

I always go to the market with Mom and Dad. We sell fruits and vegetables from our farm.

We have to get up early because
the market is far away.

As we start out this morning,
the stars are still shining.

At last we get to Red Rock. We park
the truck in the big lot and then set
up our cart.

We have lots of fruits and vegetables to sell.

"This corn smells fresh," a man says.
"These eggplants look fresh, too."

Lots of people stop at our cart.
My best friend, Carmen, stops by.

Carmen fills her arms with corn.
She gets some lemons, too.

Dad sells the last of the corn.
Now, nothing is left on the cart!

Market day is over. We pick up the trash and go back home.

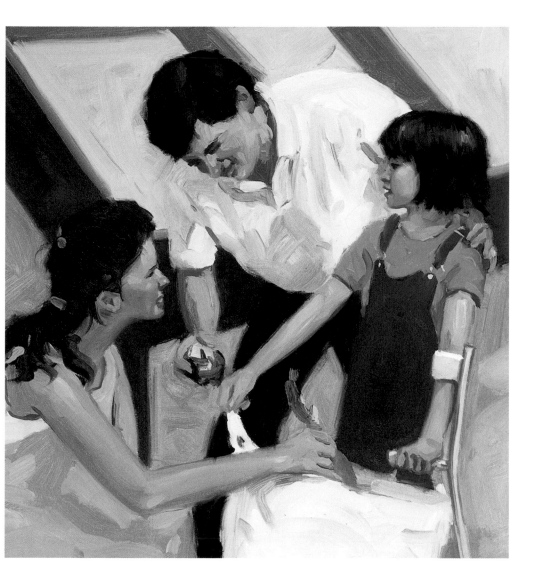

Market days always go by fast.
I think I like market days the best!

Your Own Market

Make some food to sell at your own market!

WHAT YOU'LL NEED

paper

tape

scissors

crayons or markers

1 Draw pictures of different foods. Cut them out.

2 Make some price tags. Tape them to the food.

20¢

5¢

10¢

3 Ask a friend to come to your market. Take turns buying and selling the food.

10¢

20¢

5¢

5¢

8¢

5¢

Meet the Illustrator

Edward Martinez loves to paint. He began his work on *Farmers Market* by taking pictures of real children. Then he looked at the photos as he painted the children in the story. Look closely, the kids might be based on someone you know!

Edward Martinez

www.HarcourtBooks.com

First Green Light Readers edition 2002
Green Light Readers is a trademark of Harcourt, Inc., registered in the United States of America and/or other jurisdictions.

The Library of Congress has cataloged an earlier edition as follows:
Parks, Carmen.
Farmers market/Carmen Parks; illustrated by Edward Martinez.
p. cm.
"Green Light Readers."
Summary: A girl and her parents spend the day at the farmers' market selling the vegetables they've grown.
[1. Farmers' markets—Fiction.] I. Martinez, Edward, ill. II. Title. III. Series.
PZ7.P2398Far 2002
[E]—dc21 2001002415
ISBN 0-15-204881-2
ISBN 0-15-204841-3 (pb)

A C E G H F D B
A C E G H F D B (pb)

Ages 5–7
Grades: 1–2
Guided Reading Level: G–H
Reading Recovery Level: 14–15

Green Light Readers
For the reader who's ready to GO!

"A must-have for any family with a beginning reader."—*Boston Sunday Herald*

"You can't go wrong with adding several copies of these terrific books to your beginning-to-read collection."—*School Library Journal*

"A winner for the beginner."—*Booklist*

Five Tips to Help Your Child Become a Great Reader

1. Get involved. Reading aloud to and with your child is just as important as encouraging your child to read independently.

2. Be curious. Ask questions about what your child is reading.

3. Make reading fun. Allow your child to pick books on subjects that interest her or him.

4. Words are everywhere—not just in books. Practice reading signs, packages, and cereal boxes with your child.

5. Set a good example. Make sure your child sees YOU reading.

Why Green Light Readers Is the Best Series for Your New Reader

- Created exclusively for beginning readers by some of the biggest and brightest names in children's books

- Reinforces the reading skills your child is learning in school

- Encourages children to read—and finish—books by themselves

- Offers extra enrichment through fun, age-appropriate activities unique to each story

- Incorporates characteristics of the Reading Recovery program used by educators

- Developed with Harcourt School Publishers and credentialed educational consultants

LEVEL 2 Start the Engine! Reading with Help

Daniel's Mystery Egg
Alma Flor Ada/G. Brian Karas

Animals on the Go
Jessica Brett/Richard Cowdrey

Marco's Run
Wesley Cartier/Reynold Ruffins

Digger Pig and the Turnip
Caron Lee Cohen/Christopher Denise

Tumbleweed Stew
Susan Stevens Crummel/Janet Stevens

The Chick That Wouldn't Hatch
Claire Daniel/Lisa Campbell Ernst

Splash!
Ariane Dewey/Jose Aruego

Get That Pest!
Erin Douglas/Wong Herbert Yee

Why the Frog Has Big Eyes
Betsy Franco/Joung Un Kim

I Wonder
Tana Hoban

A Bed Full of Cats
Holly Keller

The Fox and the Stork
Gerald McDermott

Boots for Beth
Alex Moran/Lisa Campbell Ernst

Catch Me If You Can!
Bernard Most

The Very Boastful Kangaroo
Bernard Most

Farmers Market
Carmen Parks/Edward Martinez

Shoe Town
Janet Stevens/Susan Stevens Crummel

The Enormous Turnip
Alexei Tolstoy/Scott Goto

Where Do Frogs Come From?
Alex Vern

The Purple Snerd
Rozanne Lanczak Williams/
Mary GrandPré

Look for more Green Light Readers wherever books are sold!